# HOTEL TRANSYLVANIA™

## The Series

PAPERCUT Z

# MORE GREAT GRAPHIC NOVEL SERIES AVAILABLE FROM PAPERCUTZ™

**THE SMURFS #21**

**THE GARFIELD SHOW #6**

**BARBIE #1**

**THE SISTERS #1**

**TROLLS #1**

**GERONIMO STILTON #17**

**THEA STILTON #6**

**SEA CREATURES #1**

**THE LUNCH WITCH #1**

**SCARLETT**

**ANNE OF GREEN BAGELS #1**

**DRACULA MARRIES FRANKENSTEIN!**

**THE RED SHOES**

**THE LITTLE MERMAID**

**FUZZY BASEBALL**

**HOTEL TRANSYLVANIA #1**

**THE LOUD HOUSE #1**

**MANOSAURS #1**

**THE ONLY LIVING BOY #5**

**GUMBY #1**

THE SMURFS, THE GARFIELD SHOW, BARBIE, HOTEL TRANSYLVANIA, MANOSAURS, THE LOUD HOUSE and TROLLS graphic novels are available for $7.99 in paperback, and $12.99 in hardcover. THE ONLY LIVING BOY and GUMBY graphic novels are available for $8.99 in paperback, and $13.99 in hardcover. GERONIMO STILTON and THEA STILTON graphic novels are available for $9.99 in hardcover only. FUZZY BASEBALL graphic novels are available for $9.99 in paperback only. THE LUNCH WITCH, SCARLETT, and ANNE OF GREEN BAGELS graphic novels are available for $14.99 in paperback only. THE RED SHOES and THE LITTLE MERMAID graphic novels are available for $12.99 in hardcover only. DRACULA MARRIES FRANKENSTEIN! graphic novels are available for $12.99 in paperback only. THE SISTERS graphic novels are available for $9.99 in paperback, and $14.99 in hardcover. SEA CREATURES graphic novels are available for $10.99 in hardcover only.

Available from booksellers everywhere. You can also order online from www.papercutz.com. Or call 1-800-886-1223, Monday through Friday, 9–5 EST. MC, Visa, and AmEx accepted. To order by mail, please add $5.00 for postage and handling for first book ordered, $1.00 for each additional book and make check payable to NBM Publishing. Send to: Papercutz, 160 Broadway, Suite 700, East Wing, New York, NY 10038.

THE SMURFS, GUMBY, THE GARFIELD SHOW, THE LOUD HOUSE, THE ONLY LIVING BOY, BARBIE, TROLLS, GERONIMO STILTON, THEA STILTON, FUZZY BASEBALL, THE LUNCH WITCH, THE LITTLE MERMAID, HOTEL TRANSYLVANIA, MANOSAURS, THE SISTERS, SEA CREATURES ,THE RED SHOES, ANNE OF GREEN BAGELS, DRACULA MARRIES FRANKENSTEIN!, and SCARLETT graphic novels are also available wherever e-books are sold.

# Hotel Transylvania
## The Series

# MY LITTLE MONSTER-SITTER

Stefan Petrucha—Writer
Allen Gladfelter
& Zazo—Artists

PAPERCUTZ
NEW YORK

# HOTEL TRANSYLVANIA
## THE SERIES

**#2 "My Little Monster-Sitter"**
**Stefan Petrucha—Writer**
**Allen Gladfelter—Penciler**
**Zazo—Inker**
**Laurie E. Smith—Colorist**
**Wilson Ramos Jr.—Letterer**
**Dawn Guzzo—Production**
**Spenser Nellis—Editorial Intern**
**Jeff Whitman—Assistant Managing Editor**
**Jim Salicrup**
**Editor-in-Chief**

**Special thanks to James Silvani, Keith Baxter, PH Marcondes, Rick Mischel, Melissa Sturm, Virginia King, and everyone at Sony Pictures Animation.**

**ISBN: 978-1-62991-855-6**

**Papercutz books may be purchased for business or promotional use.**
**For information on bulk purchases please contact Macmillan Corporate**
**and Premium Sales Department at (800) 221-795 x5442.**

Printed in China
January 2018

**Distributed by Macmillan**
**First Printing**

# MAVIS

She's the natural born leader of her friends. Mavis is 114 ¾ years old and is in full-on teenage mode: She's moody, a know-it-all, and fearless to a fault.

She's also inventive, driven, and desperate to prove she's ready for more adult responsibilities.

# HANK

Hank is the son of the scariest monster alive, the one and only Frankenstein.

He's desperate to make his mark, all in order to impress his father and get an "atta boy" out of him.

# PEDRO

Pedro acts like a kid on a permanent sugar rush.

His only purpose in life is to have fun.

Which is kind of a goal, so fine – he has one goal.

# WENDY

She is Mavis's closest contemporary and confidante. In contrast to Mavis, Wendy is shy and awkward.

She speaks with a bit of a lisp and sometimes her "s" words come with a bit of blobby spittle.

# LYDIA

Count Dracula's older sister has been summoned from 12th century Transylvania to run the Hotel, and more importantly, keep watch over Mavis in his absence. Perhaps the most evil person of the last millennium, Lydia is literally a child of the distant past and does not like change. Not only does she want to fight progress, but she wants to take the Hotel (and modern civilization, really) backwards! She despises humans, runs a tight ship, and is used to getting her way.

# WOLF PUPS

These rambunctious little pups have the run of the Hotel. Since they never stay in one place very long though, even their parents, Wayne and Wanda have lost track of how many there are!

A MESSAGE FROM THE *DEAD*-- THEY'RE ALREADY *AWAKE*, THANK YOU!

BUT, *AUNT LYDIA*, HOW ARE WE GOING TO BRING THE CASTLE *DOWN* IF WE DON'T PRACTICE?

THE CASTLE STAYS WHERE IT IS, AT LEAST WHILE YOUR FATHER IS BUSY SPEAKING AT THE *INHUMAN/HUMAN RELATIONS CONFERENCE.*

SO THIS HUMAN TRYING TO *INSULT* MY CAPE SAYS, HEY, BUDDY, HAVE YOU LOOKED IN A *MIRROR* LATELY?

AND, I SAID, *SURE*, BUT I *CAN'T* SEE A THING!

BECAUSE, Y'KNOW....!

SHAVING CAN BE A *PAIN.* AM I RIGHT?

HA-HA-HA-HA-HA!

MAVIS, YOU'RE NEEDED TO *PUPPY-SIT* WANDA AND WAYNE'S RAMBUNCTIOUS OFFSPRING!

SEE TO IT THAT NONE OF THEM GET *LOST!*

WE *WILL* BE COUNTING!

POOF

THAT DOESN'T SOUND SO BAD, I *LIKE* THE PUPS.

AND HEY, SOMEONE WITH *BEETLES* CAN'T REALLY COMPLAIN ABOUT FLEAS!

AS LONG AS THEY DON'T NIBBLE AT YOUR STITCHES!

LYDIA ONLY *THINKS* THEY'RE WILD BECAUSE SHE CAN'T REMEMBER WHAT IT'S LIKE TO BE LESS THAN A *THOUSAND* YEARS OLD. BUT I DO!

YOU JUST HAVE TO KEEP 'EM BUSY WITH COOL GAMES! I STILL REMEMBER MY DAD AND I PLAYING *CREEP-A-BOO* WITH A REAL GHOST.

CREEP-A...

BOO!

I'M SURE THOSE DOGS'LL DIG *MY* FAVORITE KIDDIE GAME...

BODY TAG!

PEDRO, YOU'RE *IT*-- THE THING FROM OUTER SPACE!

OR MINE... HIDE AND SHRIEK!

FOUND YOU, WENDY!

AIIIEEE!

WHAT AM I THINKING? IT'S NOT *JUST* ABOUT ENTERTAINMENT! I COULD INFLUENCE THEIR *WHOLE* LIVES!

OF *COURSE* WE'LL SIT STILL FOR *YOU*, MAVIS!

WE *KNOW* IF WE LISTEN FOR A FEW SECONDS, WE'LL HAVE FUN FOR A *LIFETIME!*

WHO KNEW FINGERLESS-PAINTING COULD BE SO *EXCITING?*

*PIN THE EYE ON THE CYCLOPS* IS THE BEST GAME IN THE MONSTER WORLD! YOU'RE A MAD GENIUS, MAVIS!

I WISH YOU COULD SIT US *FOREVER!*

THANKS TO *ME*, THEY COULD BECOME THE PRIDE AND JOY OF THE MONSTER WORLD!

EVIL RAY

DED TALKS

THANKS! I REALLY DESERVE THIS *AWARD!*

BEST EVAH

OH, BATS! I SOUND JUST LIKE *LYDIA!*

I'VE GOT TO BE MORE CREATIVE THAN THAT!

WHO WANTS THE STICK? WHO WANTS IT, HUH?

YOU ALL DO, YES, YOU DO!

THEN SIT UP AND LISTEN!

I'M GOING TO BE SITTING FOR YOU TODAY, SO...

A SITTER?

NOOOOO!

WE'RE TOO COOL FOR A SITTER!

CAN WE KIDNAP YOU AND LEAVE YOU IN THE LAKE LIKE THE LAST ONE?

MAYBE SOME OF THE LITTLE SCAMPS ARE IN HERE.

IF I COULD JUST...GET IT... OPEN!

CRRRRKK

CLOSE THE LID!

OH, SORRY!

SORRY, DIDN'T KNOW IT WAS OCCUPIED.

IS ALRIGHT.

⇌PHEW!⇌ LOOKING FOR THOSE PUPS IS DRIVING ME BATS!

SPEAKING OF WHICH, I'LL COVER MORE GROUND FROM THE AIR!

POOF

MY SPIN... *BAD.*

IT'S THE LARGEST BONE IN THE BODY! YOU MAY AS WELL GIVE UP, NOW, HANK!

WHOA! YOU HAVE TO EXTRACT THE FEMUR!

I CAN *DO* THIS! I *KNOW* I CAN!

ALMOST GOT IT! ALMOST.... ALMOST...

GO, HANK! GO, HANK! GO, HANK!

GUYS! GUYS! GUYS!

YOW!

CRASH

ALMOST. ⸮SOB�od; ALMOST.

WOW, WAS THAT A *SET-UP* FOR A JOKE OR WHAT?

YEAH, GOOD THING WE WEREN'T CARRYING A HUGE PILE OF *PLATES*, OR A SHEET OF *GLASS* OR SOMETHING.

FUNNY YOU MENTION THAT. I HIT *BOTH* ON MY WAY HERE.

SORRY, BUT THE PUPS HAVE GONE *AHOWL* IN THE CATACOMBS AND I NEED YOUR HELP FINDING THEM!

POOF

A-WHAT?

AWAY FROM *HOME* AND *OVERJOYED* TO BE *WITHOUT* LEASHES!

I'M SURE THEY CAN TAKE CARE OF THEMSELVES, BUT I *HAVE* TO FIND THEM BEFORE AUNT LYDIA FINDS OUT I'VE BLOWN IT!

WE'LL HELP, BUT, HEY, WHAT'S THE *WORST* THAT CAN HAPPEN?

FAILURE

OH, YOU'D BE SURPRISED...

IT'S OKAY, HANK, BUT THERE ARE *SOME* PLACES WE *CAN'T* ALL GET TO.

LIKE *THIS!*

NO BONES ABOUT IT, YOU CAN GET INTO THE *DARNDEST* PLACES IF YOU DON'T *HAVE* BONES!

HUH. THIS LOOKS LIKE *DR. GILMAN'S* OLD WAITING ROOM!

≶*BRR!*≶ I STILL REMEMBER HIS *COLD* STETHOSCOPE! LAST TIME I HAD A PHYSICAL, IT WAS STUCK IN MY CHEST SO BADLY, IT TOOK AN *HOUR* TO GET IT OUT

UH-OH! *THIS* CAN'T BE GOOD!

*GREAT!* I'M *OOZING* THROUGH THIS GRATE.

WE'D LIKE YOU TO BE OUR QUEEN!

WHY, THANK-YOU! THAT IS SO NICE!

BUT...UH...THIS IS ALL HAPPENING SO FAST!

AND I'VE NEVER BEEN A QUEEN BEFORE! I'M NOT SURE I'D KNOW WHAT TO DO!

YOU DON'T DO ANYTHING!

WE DO IT ALL FOR YOU!

HMM. THAT, I THINK I CAN HANDLE!

GOTCHA!

WHEE!

TAG!

GOT YOU LAST!

LOOK AT ME!

NO FAIR!

IT'S ALL FAIR DOWN HERE!

RUN FROM *ME*, WILL YOU? BUT YOU DIDN'T COUNT ON... **THE REVENGE OF THE MONSTER-SITTER!**

**BWAH-HA-HA!**

I DUNNO. THEY'RE SO DARN *CUTE!*

AND IT SEEMS A *SHAME* TO INTERRUPT ALL THAT WILD, CRAZY FUN.

YEAH, YEAH! BUT IF *LYDIA* FINDS OUT I MESSED UP, I'LL NEVER SEE THE OTHER LIGHT OF THE MOON AGAIN!

SO, YOU TWO GO AROUND TO THE OTHER SIDE AND *BLOCK* THE OTHER EXITS! I'LL DEAL WITH THE PUPS!

OKAY, OKAY!

GOT IT?

HEY! DON'T YOU REALIZE I'M IN CHARGE HERE?

WAIT. DON'T ANSWER THAT.

RUNNING AROUND AND PLAYING WITH NO RULES, HUH? THAT DOES LOOK KIND OF *GREAT!*

I HEAR THAT. IT'S LIKE AN ANCIENT CALL TO MY INNER WILD!

AFTER ALL, *HAPPINESS* IS A WARM WERE-PUPPY HORDE!

AW! THE LITTLE GUYS ARE TAKING ME FOR A *SPIN!*

**STOP!**

46

BEING FERAL'S GREAT!

WHAT DOES FERAL MEAN EXACTLY?

OH, WHO CARES?

AS LONG AS WE GET TO ACT WILD!

GUYS?

MAY I *PLEASE* TALK TO YOU ALL FOR A SECOND?

NO!

WE'RE BUSY BEING FERAL!

IGNORE HER.

MAYBE SHE'LL GO AWAY.

EVEN IF I SHOW YOU...THIS?

OH... *MY.*

IT LOOKS SO... WOODY.

BET IT FEELS *GREAT* TO CHEW ON!

NOT *THIS* TIME!

WE'VE GOT *SOME* SELF-CONTROL!

NAH!

AND IT'S NOT LIKE YOU'RE A SQUIRREL.

OH, YEAH? HOW ABOUT...

A BIG RED *BALL!*

WHO WANTS TO CATCH IT? WHO DOES? *WHO?*

I DO!

I DO!

I DO!

HEY, YOU'RE NOT GOING TO TRY TO BLOCK OFF THE EXITS AGAIN, ARE YOU?

OR WORSE, *PRETEND* TO THROW IT WHILE YOU'RE REALLY *KEEPING* IT IN YOUR HAND? I *HATE* THAT!

I DON'T KNOW WHAT YOU'RE THINKING, BUT I NEED YOU TO UNDERSTAND SOMETHING.

I'M ONLY HERE TO GIVE YOU *ONE* MORE CHANCE TO COME HOME.

BEFORE IT'S TOO *LATE!*

NO, I MEAN THERE ARE THINGS LIVING DOWN HERE THAT EVEN MONSTERS FEAR!

TOO LATE?

I LOVE IT WHEN IT'S LATE!

NO BEDTIME WHEN YOU'RE FERAL!

FEH!

WE'RE WEREWOLVES!

WHAT COULD SCARE US?

THINGS LIKE THE DREADED...

WERE-PUP EATERS!

GATHER ROUND AND I'LL *TELL* YOU ABOUT THEM!

THEN DO WE GET THE BALL?

WHOA!

WHILE YOU SLEEP?

THAT IS SO CREEPY!

HA!

YOU MUST THINK WE'RE SUCKERS!

YOU'RE JUST MAKING THAT UP!

THINK I'M MAKING IT UP, DO YOU?

SURE YOU ARE!

GIANT CATS!

I MEAN, REALLY!

UH... UH...

LEAVE THE BALL, BUT GO HOME!

WE'RE NO SAPS!

GO HOME, MAVIS!

UH! UH! UH! UH! UH!

BWA-HAHAHAHAH!

DID YOU SEE THEM *RUN!*

HA! YOU MAY NOT BE A GREAT SITTER...

HEH-HEH. ...BUT YOU'RE A *MONSTER* STORY-TELLER!

THANKS SO MUCH, YOU GUYS! BUT I THINK IT'S TIME *WE* WERE HEADED BACK HOME, TOO!

HOME? BUT WE WANT YOU TO *STAY* HERE AS OUR QUEEN!

SORRY! I REALLY *CAN'T!*

MUCH AS I LIKE BEING QUEEN, I'D MISS MY HOME AND MY *FRIENDS!*

OH, *THEY* CAN COME TOO!

THEY CAN BE OUR QUEEN AND KINGS, TOO!

BUT...HOW CAN YOU HAVE MORE THAN *ONE* QUEEN OR KING?

SIMPLE!

EVERY WEEK, WE TAKE OUR KING AND QUEEN...

AND *EAT* THEM!

AHHHHHHHHHH!

# THE END

# WATCH OUT FOR PAPERCUTZ™

Welcome to the frightful final pages of HOTEL TRANSYLVANIA #2 "My Little Monster-Sitter," the gruesome giggle-inducing graphic novel by "Spooky" Stefan Petrucha, writer, and Allen "Ghostly" Gladfelter and Zazo "the Zombie," artists, from "Petrifying" Papercutz—those batty boys and ghouls dedicated to publishing great graphic novels for all ages. I'm Jim "Screaming" Salicrup, Editor-in-Chief and Substitute Bellhop at the HOTEL TRANSYLVANIA. I'm here to once again share a personal behind-the-scenes story and recommend a few Papercutz graphic novels. First, the behind-the-scenes story…

As a kid growing up a long, long time ago, I was always looking for ways to earn a little extra money. You see, I was addicted to comicbooks, and every week I had to get another fix. (I still do! Just ask Ted and Ingrid at my favorite comicbook store.) And for that I needed moolabux, dough, *mucho dinero*—in other words, cold hard cash. After all, a comicbook was about 12 cents an issue back then, 25 cents for the double-size annuals (I told you it was a long, long time ago). I did whatever I could to supplement my 25-cents-a-week allowance. I carried grocery bags for tips. I shined shoes. I searched for deposit bottles to cash in. But my favorite gig was babysitting. One of my neighbors would hire me to baby sit their infant son, and I'd have their whole apartment to myself— and the best part was, the father was a comics fan who worked downtown, and he'd get the new comics a full week ahead of when they would arrive in the neighborhood. The kid was a real dream to take care of compared to Wanda and Wayne's wolf pups, but still, with great power must also come great responsibility, and I'm proud to say, there was never any mishaps, and everything turned out well.

Speaking of old comicbooks, Papercutz has probably published the most unexpected comics revival of the year—MANOSAURS! Two virtually forgotten comicbooks, MANOSAURS #0 (Yeah, that was a thing!) and #1, were published back in the 1900s—1993 to be precise. The MANOSAURS were created by Stuart Fischer, and was about these out-of-time characters that were published way ahead of their time. Now the MANOSAURS are back, courtesy of "Spooky" Stefan Petrucha, writer, and Yellowhale, artists. MANOSAURS is the story of Denise and Leo "Doc" Jeffries, down on their luck proprietors of the dumpy

Dynamic Dino Display museum, and what happens when "Doc" unearths a box of bona fide dinosaur eggs in their backyard. These eggs hatch four talking dinosaurs that rapidly adapt and grow into their new environment, becoming Tri, Rex, Ptor, and Pterry, human/dinosaur hybrids called MANOSAURS, with the personalities of typical teenagers. MANOSAURS is available now at your favorite booksellers. Check out the preview on the following pages.

Back to HOTEL TRANSYLVANIA, we're sure you noticed that this time around we're offering up an all-new story based on HOTEL TRANSYLVANIA THE SERIES. In HOTEL TRANSYLVANIA #3, we'll be back to presenting a new story inspired by the movie series. It's called "Motel Transylvania," and wait till you see why! We hope you enjoyed your stay at HOTEL TRANSYLVANIA and hope you return soon.

Thanks,

Jim

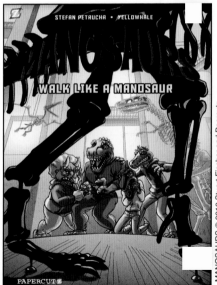

## STAY IN TOUCH!

EMAIL: salicrup@papercutz.com
WEB: papercutz.com
INSTAGRAM: @papercutzgn
TWITTER: @papercutzgn
FACEBOOK: PAPERCUTZGRAPHICNOVELS
FAN MAIL: Papercutz, 160 Broadway, Suite 700, East Wing, New York, NY 10038

**MANOSAURS #1 "Walk Like a Manosaur!"**
**is available at booksellers everywhere.**